INDIGO WILDE

AND THE CREATURES AT JELLYBEAN CRESCENT

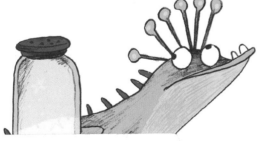

Pippa Curnick

INDIGO WILDE

AND THE CREATURES AT JELLYBEAN CRESCENT

HODDER CHILDREN'S BOOKS

First published in Great Britain in 2021 by Hodder & Stoughton
This paperback edition published in 2022

1 3 5 7 9 10 8 6 4 2

ISBN 978 1 444 94882 0

Printed and bound in China

The paper and board used in this book are made from wood from
responsible sources

Hodder Children's Books
An imprint of Hachette Children's Group
Part of Hodder & Stoughton Limited
Carmelite House
50 Victoria Embankment
London EC4Y 0DZ
An Hachette UK Company
www.hachette.co.uk
www.hachettechildrens.co.uk

This book is dedicated to these exceptional explorers:

AUTUMN: CAT WRANGLER

BEN: MONSTER TAMER

ROUX: DRAGON RIDER

KING WELLINGTON

The Daily Waffle

SECRET NEWS FOR EXPLORERS OF UNKNOWN WORLDS

TUESDAY 9TH OCTOBER

WORLD-FAMOUS EXPLORERS PHILOMENA & BERTRAM WILDE SAVE BABY FROM TOOTHSOME TIGER

LAST TUESDAY, JUST AFTER TEATIME, World-Famous Explorers Philomena and Bertram Wilde discovered a baby crawling through the Jungliest Jungle of the Unknown Wilderness. The nine-month-old was being stalked by a huge and toothsome tiger

and would have been gobbled up had it not been for the Wildes' quick thinking. With little care for her own safety, Mrs Wilde wrestled the tiger to the ground and glued its jaws shut (temporarily) with a handy tube of Dr Gnasher's Extra Sticky Superglue.

Mr Wilde tied the tiger's paws together with its own tail, boffed it on the nose with his shoe and gave the hungry baby his last egg sandwich.

The Wildes plan to adopt the baby girl if they cannot find her birth parents. The wisdom of bringing a baby into their

home, however, is yet to be seen.

MY DAD IS A UNICORN!
FULL STORY ON PAGE 25

It has been known for many years (amongst

those of us who venture to explore the strange and magical Unknown Worlds) that the Wildes' house at 47 Jellybean Crescent, Boggy Bottom, England is home to a variety of exotic and dangerous Creatures. The Wildes are well known for rescuing these Creatures if they have been injured or cast out of their natural homes, and providing them with a safe place to recuperate.

Just last month, THE DAILY WAFFLE reported that the Wildes had invited a goblin to live at number 47.

Mrs Wilde told our reporter that the goblin had been cast out of her

DR GNASHER'S
EXTRA STICKY
SUPERGLUE
STRONGEST GLUE IN
THE UNKNOWN WORLD!

family home because she had been secretly eating potato salad, rather than a goblin's usual fare of small children.

Mr Wilde told us that the goblin will become a permanent resident at 47 and 'will be a wonderful babysitter.'

With their ever-expanding menagerie of strange, magical and undoubtedly dangerous Creatures, (and now with a new baby in tow) the Wildes need to tread very carefully — it seems like only a

IS YOUR HOUSE A STINKY PIT?
THEN YOU NEED...
MRS BRISTLEBOTTOM'S
Stubborn Stain & Stench Remover

matter of time before the other inhabitants of Jellybean Crescent start to notice that something strange is going on, and everyone in the Unknown World knows that would lead to all sorts of terrible trouble.

–ONE–
47 Jellybean Crescent

Indigo Wilde was a normal eleven-year-old. Mostly. She liked doughnuts and ice skating and her little brother, Quigley, but she wasn't so keen on maths, or hoovering, or homework.

There *were* a few things that were unusual about Indigo: her family, for a

1

start. Indigo's parents, Philomena and Bertram Wilde, were World-Famous Explorers. They travelled all over the Known and Unknown World searching for new and dangerous Creatures. The Wildes loved anything crawly or beastly or furry or scaly – and if it could breathe fire or eat a person whole, all the better. Not only had Indigo's parents rescued her from a terrible man-eating tiger, they had also saved her little brother.

Quigley had only been a tiny baby when Philomena and Bertram had found him in a dragon's nest halfway up an erupting volcano. But he had not escaped unscathed; the dragon's roars had been so deafeningly loud that Quigley had lost his hearing. Quigley was the smartest person Indigo knew and before long the whole family could talk in sign language.

The problem with having parents that were World-Famous Explorers was that they weren't at home very much. They were always getting called away on Important Expeditions, so Indigo and Quigley often had to look after the house and all the magical Creatures that lived there.

This was usually quite fun because they got to eat mountains of ice cream and stay up past their bedtimes, but sometimes being left in charge was a bit annoying. For instance, they could never invite friends over for sleepovers in case they got eaten by a goblin.

Indigo and Quigley lived at number 47 Jellybean Crescent. The street itself was fairly ordinary – the road was the usual boring grey colour, there were a few spindly trees and a regiment of lamp posts along the pavement.

If you'd looked a little closer, though, which people rarely do, you'd have seen that the tree outside number 47 was a little bit different: its branches were twisted and knotted into funny shapes, which made it look like a gnarled and weatherbeaten old monster.

If you'd looked closer still, you'd have noticed that the stretch of boring grey road outside number 47 sparkled, as if tiny diamonds had been mixed into the tarmac.

And if you'd squeezed your eyes really, really tight, squinted very, very hard and wiggled your eyebrows up and down, you'd have seen that the lamplight outside number 47 glowed with the faintest hint of green.

Number 47 was ginormous. Indigo wasn't even sure she'd been in all the rooms yet and she'd lived there for years.

Indigo loved the house so much it made her chest ache. She loved that, although every other house on the street was small and boxy and the beige colour of stale bread crusts, number 47 was a mad riot of pink and green and blue and orange that made your eyes water.

She loved that her house had circular windows, star-shaped windows and windows with multicoloured panes. She especially liked the huge stained-glass window on the eighth floor with a picture of a unicorn on it. She loved the turrets, the overgrown garden filled with pixies, the library where the herd of snortlephants lived and the greenhouse bursting with man-eating plants.

The house had sixteen chimneys that stuck out of the many roofs in all directions, and Indigo loved each and every one. Some were shaped like corkscrews, there was one that puffed out rainbow-coloured smoke, and Indigo's favourite were the pink chimneys on the third floor that sang 'Jingle Bells' every time a fire was lit below.

On the sixth floor, a flock of glittery glamingos (similar to flamingos, but much more fabulous) had made sparkling nests. Perched high up on the very tippity-top roof was a rusty old weathervane shaped like a pig eating a sandwich, which spun this way

and that even when there was no wind to speak of.

All in all, number 47 was not a normal house. The most not-normal thing about it, though, was that nobody seemed to notice how not-normal it was. The people who lived on Jellybean Crescent didn't look at Indigo's house and think, "My, my, what a funny house!" or ask, "Why is there a pig eating a sandwich on that roof?" No, they mostly just ignored it, shutting themselves inside their boxy beige houses without giving a second thought to this extraordinary house on their impossibly ordinary street.

The spectacular house stood, ignored by the rest of the inhabitants of Jellybean Crescent – until one Saturday in June, when things started to go a little bit wrong …

-TWO-
A SPECIAL DELIVERY

Indigo Wilde had been awake since before
the sun came up. She had already been out
into the garden in her wellington boots
to dig up buckets of worms for the flocks
of magical birds, watered the man-eating
plants and delivered bowls of slugs'-breath
porridge, pickled bogey broth and scrambled
eggs to the goblins, trolls and yetis.

Indigo had just put fresh hay in the
basement for the llama-corn (who was on

a strict diet after eating half the contents of her mother's wardrobe), and was spooning snot-flakes into a baby troll's mouth, when the doorbell rang. Indigo's doorbell wasn't one of those nice musical ones you get in ordinary houses; it was a big rusty old clanger that made your teeth rattle in your head, so when it rang it made Indigo jump and spill the snot flakes down her T-shirt.

Scrubbing at the green slime with an old sock that had been drying limply on the radiator, she opened the door to the postman. He looked confused, as he often did when delivering to Indigo's house, and handed her two boxes before running pell-mell down the street, shrieking his head off. Indigo thought this was a *bit* of an overreaction – the biting daises on the front step had only taken a *tiny* chunk out of his shoe.

Indigo took the boxes into the kitchen, where Quigley was munching his way through his third jar of marmalade, dolloping great orangey blobs of it on his toast. She opened the smaller parcel and saw it contained several bars of exotic-looking chocolate.

Indigo sighed. She thought that chocolate tasted of old socks and mud, but her parents kept sending it as a souvenir from whichever crazy country they happened to be exploring and she didn't have the heart to tell them she didn't like it. The result was that she had a box in her bedroom bulging with chocolate treats – and she couldn't even invite her friends over to eat any of it, in case they got sat on by a dragon.

Quigley licked his lips. (Another perk of their parents being away a lot was being able to have chocolate for breakfast without any grown-ups telling him off.)

"Mum and Dad have sent us some Monster Mail, look!" Indigo said excitedly, showing Quigley the bigger box. It was made of metal with air holes in the lid and sides and had "DANGEROUS

CREATURE" and "HANDLE WITH CARE" and "FLAMMABLE" stamped all over the outside.

Philomena and Bertram often sent Creatures home via Monster Mail. The Creatures arrived in big boxes or crates. The problem was, they very rarely remembered to warn Indigo, so the deliveries always came as a bit of a surprise. Once Quigley had opened the front door to get the milk in and found a dragon sitting on the doorstep and the porch reduced to ashes.

At first, Indigo had wondered why her parents kept all these Creatures. Surely they'd do better in the wild? But it hadn't taken her very long to realise that the Creatures her parents sent home were all a bit … different. Just like her and Quigley, some had no parents of their own and needed love and care. Some had been cast out of their herds or flocks or swarms for being the wrong colour, the wrong size or the wrong shape.

For one reason or another the Creatures that lived at number 47 just didn't fit in. The house had become a place – a sanctuary of sorts – where they could belong, without being stared at or bullied for being different. And *that* was what Indigo loved most of all about the house.

"I wonder what it could be this time?" Indigo said, using her hands to sign to Quigley. "Maybe it's a baby dragon, or a skull-squishing sneezle. Hmm, no, the box is too small. Reckon it's another flying monkey? Or a fairy?"

"RAAAAAR!" roared Quigley, gnashing his teeth, crossing his eyes and pretending to be a terrifying marmalade-dripping monster.

"Gosh, I hope not," replied Indigo, laughing.

"I've got far too much stuff to do today without having a monster to look after. Let's hope it's something nice and quiet and *easy*."

She heaved the lid open and peered inside. There was a pile of straw, a few crinkled, empty chocolate wrappers and half an envelope that looked like it had been

chewed by sharp teeth, but nothing else. No gnashing jaws, scratching claws or beady eyes. In fact, the only other thing in the box was a large hole straight out the other side.

"It's chewed straight through the metal!" Quigley signed, sticking his head through the hole and pulling a grotesque face.

Indigo and Quigley looked at each other, worried. Whatever had been in the package was not there now, so it was probably either loose in the house, or loose in the post office. Indigo wasn't sure which was worse … She was fairly certain the postman's nerves couldn't cope with having a monster rampaging around his mail room but, on the other hand, she and Quigley had only just got the house sorted after their parents' last special delivery.

Last month, Philomena and Bertram had

sent two yeti twins called Olli and Umpf. Indigo and Quigley had quickly made the yetis feel at home with large bowls of ice cream (with chocolate sauce, sprinkles and an eyeball on top). Unfortunately, the ice cream had given the yetis terrible brain freeze so Indigo and Quigley had spent the next two hours chasing the twins all over the house, trying to stop them smashing walls down in an ice-cream-fuelled frenzy.

Trying to shake off this unpleasant memory, Indigo picked up the scrap of envelope and saw it had her name on the front in her mother's handwriting. There were only a few tiny pieces of the letter left inside and they weren't very useful at all ...

Dear Indigo,

Very hot here. Found this

He's really easy to

Your father has sunburn on his

Have fun!

Love, Mum and Dad x

Indigo crumpled up the scraps and sighed. Quigley shrugged with disappointment and went back to his marmalade. They would just have to hope this particular Creature had found its way back to wherever it had come from.

Indigo checked the kitchen clock. "I'm just going to go and see if I can find you some matching socks," she signed to Quigley.

But before she could make her way upstairs, she noticed that the parcel containing the chocolate was now empty. Quigley had a funny look on his face.

"Quigley, have you eaten all that chocolate? Crumping crumpets, you'll be sick!"

Quigley shook his head and pointed into the hall. He signed with such speed that his hands were almost a blur.

"I can't understand if you talk too quickly," grumbled Indigo. "Just don't eat anything else or you won't have room for lunch. I'm making salad."

Quigley folded his arms, looking cross. But Indigo wasn't sure if that was because she'd told him off about the chocolate, or because no self-respecting five-year-old can get excited about eating salad. Indigo hurried out of the room and started to climb the winding stairs, cheerfully greeting the Creatures she met on the way.

"Morning, Olli. Morning, Umpf!" she called to the yetis, who were playing croquet in the hallway. "Your fur is looking lovely this morning." It had been immediately obvious to Indigo why her parents had sent Olli and Umpf to number 47 – their shaggy fur was luminous pink and blue, instead of the usual white. It was much harder to jump out and gobble up unsuspecting skiers when your fur was as bright as Olli's and Umpf's.

"Oh, hello, Graham," Indigo added weakly as the llama-corn bounced past her, chomping madly on a pair of pink bloomers. "Oi, you're supposed to be on a diet!" she called after him, but he'd bounced away.

Sighing, she carried on, humming as
she climbed staircase after staircase. There
didn't seem to be a monster on the loose.
Everything seemed quite normal, or as
normal as it ever got at number 47. She
met Queenie the goblin on the third floor,
looking even more ferocious than usual.
She had her large bottom in the air and was
throwing her possessions out of her drawers
and on to the landing.

"Morning, Queenie. Are you all right?
Need a hand with anything?" Indigo asked.

"I've lost me blinkin' bloomers. They're
my best pink ones – you seen 'em? Sure
I'd put them in here, but they've gone,"
Queenie snarled, gnashing her sharp little
teeth.

"Ah ... er ... no," said Indigo, "well ...
good luck finding them.

I'll let you know if they … er … turn up."

Everything in the house seemed to be in order, Indigo thought as she fished a pair of socks out of Quigley's drawer. No sign of an escaped monster of any sort.

Then, from far below, there was an almighty crash followed by an almightier

MEOOOOWWWWWW

WWWWWWW

THE SOUND

OF

A

VERY

ANGRY

PURRMAID...

-THREE-

THE GREAT LOO FLOOD

A purrmaid, if you don't already know, has the top half of a cat and the bottom half of a fish. You might be able to see one for yourself if you go to the beach at midnight, stand on your head in a rock pool and recite the alphabet backwards. Then again, you might not. They are quite rare.

The purrmaid living in Indigo's bathroom was called Fishkins and he was extra-specially GRUMPY. His cat half was ginger and fluffy and bigger than a tiger. His fish tail had shiny blue scales and was so large it hung over the edge of the bath, where he spent most of his time. Fishkins had lived at number 47 for a decade and he got grumpier and grumpier every day. The reason for his bad mood was simple – the cat part of him HATED water, but the fish part of him LOVED it. He spent his whole day soaking his fish tail, trying not to get his fur wet and grumbling whenever anyone came in to use the loo.

Indigo crashed down the stairs. The deafening MEEEEEEOOWWW was coming straight from Fishkins' bathroom, and so was the unmistakable sloshing sound of water.

Indigo raced down the hall. The bathroom door was rattling on its hinges and water was spurting out from the crack underneath.

"What on earth is going on in there,

Fishkins?" called out Indigo.

Just as she lifted her hand to grab the handle, the door burst open with an ear-splitting WHOOSH and out flooded a gigantic wave of freezing-cold water. On the crest of the wave, meowing and hissing at the top of his lungs, was Fishkins in his bathtub, bobbing up and down like a sailing boat on a stormy sea.

The wave crashed through the hallway, water spurting from the pipes where the bathtub had once been connected. Fishkins sloshed around the house in a whirlpool of foaming bubbles, knocking pictures from the walls. Quigley bobbed into view, riding high in Queenie's arms, clutching his toast in one hand and wielding a croquet mallet like a sword in the other. He was laughing merrily, clearly having the time of his life.

Indigo grabbed hold of a wall light and hauled herself out of the deluge and on to a bookcase. She caught hold of Quigley's croquet mallet, pulling her brother on to the bookcase as Queenie tried to swim after Fishkins. The poor purrmaid was being tossed this way and that by the rolling waves, meowing in rage.

Just when Indigo thought the situation couldn't get any worse, the yeti twins came careening down the stairs, banging their great pink and blue chests.

"'ONSTER! 'ONSTER UP!" they bellowed, pointing up the stairs.

"Monster? What sort of monster?" called Indigo, but the yetis had run straight into the swirling torrents and were howling so loudly no one could hear a thing. Indigo managed to pull

Olli on to the bookcase, but Umpf thrashed her arms around in panic as the flood swirled and twirled her about. Quigley hopped up and down, pointing at the front door.

"Open the front door! Open the front door!" Indigo shouted, but no matter how hard Umpf tried, she just couldn't get close enough to the door to open it. She crashed into the grandfather clock with a loud BONG! and smashed into a large (and very ugly) ornamental vase, sending a huge cloud of giant moths skywards. Eventually, with a ginormous CRASH, she bashed her way straight through the front wall of the house. The water, the yeti, the goblin and the yowling purrmaid went cascading through the giant hole and out into the jungle of a garden.

"Well, that did the trick," shrugged Indigo, as Quigley dived into the sloshing waves and was swept away, laughing, as if he was on a water flume at a theme park.

In all the chaos it took quite a long time for Indigo to get any sense out of anyone. First, she had to stop Quigley from surfing around the bathroom on an old baking tray, then she had to persuade a couple of trolls to take turns sitting on the spurting water pipes until she could find the telephone number for a plumber. The yeti twins took a long time to calm down and she had to read them two bedtime stories *each* to get them to stop yowling. Quigley mopped the floor with the help of a gang of pixies, and Indigo made everyone a cup of tea. Queenie emerged to help patch up the wall and rehang the pictures (she was still muttering about losing her bloomers) and Graham enthusiastically rounded up the giant moths with a net.

Fishkins refused to say a single word until Indigo had dried him thoroughly with a hairdryer and put his fur in rollers. When the purrmaid's fur had been coiffed and he'd been settled on the comfiest chair, his tail wrapped in wet flannels and a glass of warm milk in his paw, he spoke.

"It was a MONSTER!" Fishkins exploded. "It was as tall as a house. It burst right in, stole my scrambled eggs, lifted the bath clean off the floor and ripped the pipes out. It was all *most* undignified." He threw his paw over his eyes for dramatic effect.

"But what did the monster look like? Did it say anything?" asked Indigo desperately.

"Didn't see," replied Fishkins unhelpfully, his nose in the air. "It was all over in a blur."

Quigley did some elaborate sign language.

"What do you mean you saw something? You didn't tell me!" Indigo cried.

Quigley signed, twirling his hands around crossly before putting them on his hips, looking grumpy.

"Oh, you tried to tell me at breakfast? Sorry, Quig. But you didn't actually see it? Just a flash of blue fire? And it ate the *chocolate* Mum and Dad sent?" Indigo frowned. "I've never come across a Creature that eats chocolate before … unless you count Graham, but he eats anything if it stays still long enough. Hmm. I think I need to consult the *Abracadarium*."

Quigley's eyes grew wide with excitement.

"Can I go now?" Fishkins huffed impatiently. "You'll have to carry me back to the bathroom before my tail dries out. It's a lot of effort to keep it this shiny, you know." He swished his huge tail, splattering everyone with wet flannels.

-FOUR-
THE ABRACADARIUM

Once Fishkins had been carried back to
his bathroom, Indigo left Quigley painting
Queenie's claws and hurried up to her
bedroom. She closed the door and sank on
to her bed with a sigh. She had so many
cushions and blankets that it felt like being
inside a giant squishy nest.

Opposite her bed there was an enormous,
draughty old window that nearly took up
the whole wall. It had a star-shaped pane

at the very top in deepest yellow and pink
stained glass and blue swirls of rippled glass
disappearing into white glass clouds. The
sun was shining and it bounced beautiful
shards of colour all around the room. Indigo
often sat by the window, drawing in her
sketchbook and planning all the adventures
she would go on when she didn't have to
go to school any more. She had a brilliant
view of the overgrown back garden (where,
today, Horace the dragon was snoozing in
the sunshine) and into the fields and woods
beyond.

Indigo reached down and pulled a box
out from underneath her bed. She plonked
it on to her duvet and opened it. Inside
was a huge mound of chocolate sent by her
parents, all with different and exotic-looking
wrappers. Underneath the chocolate, at the

very bottom of the box was a large book bound in dark leather and with fancy gold letters on the front saying *Abracadarium*.

"Now, let's see," she muttered to herself as she carefully turned the dusty old pages. The book was ancient and had that lovely mildewy smell of aged paper. Each page had beautiful drawings of the most fantastical Creatures and information in elaborate curly writing.

The *Abracadarium* had been written by her great-great-great-grandmother, Gertrude Wilde, who had been a formidable and brilliant woman. She had once sailed across the Frosty Sea in an old bathtub and, when she'd got tired of rowing, had lassoed a couple of sharks to tow her the rest of the way. Over the years many people had scribbled useful extra titbits in the margins so that there was barely a blank space left.

Indigo turned to the section on fire-breathing Creatures, but there were only two entries … Dragon (various species) and Chimera.

Fire-breathers

Various species.
For water dragons see page 2498
For mountain dragons see page 1283

DRAGON
(FIRE SPECIES)

Highly aggressive
species - will breathe
fire on sight.

SIZE: LARGE (5 TONNES)

PINK FIRE

BLUE TONGUE

Vivid pink scales

Small wings - gliding

I rode a fire dragon once. Nearly singed my socks off. Gertrude Wilde (14)

Blue horns + spikes

DISTRIBUTION: Volcanic islands
DIET: Lava for fire production
Large mammals

CHIMERA

Very rare - only 1
known in existence.
Unpredictable - can
attack without warning
DISTRIBUTION: Greek islands
SIZE: LARGE   DIET: mixed

Lion sly

goat stubborn

snake can be aggressive

Whatever had come in that box was definitely neither of those. Indigo flopped back on her bed, trying to remember any tips from her parents, but her brain was blank. She stared at the paintings and pictures hanging in mismatched frames above her bed. Indigo's favourite was the huge family portrait that they had been given by Henri Herringbone, a famous painter that her parents had once rescued from the stomach of a giant trout. Henri had captured Quigley perfectly – the toddler was visible as just a pair of upside-down legs sticking up from the bottom of the painting.

Indigo remembered that Quigley had seen a beetle on the floor so instead of sitting still to be painted, he had launched himself face first on to the carpet to retrieve the treasure.

The other excellent thing about the
painting was that Henri had painted her
mother mid-sneeze.

Thinking of Henri Herringbone and
his trout, Indigo sat up and opened the
Abracadarium again, this time
at the water-dwelling Creatures.

Water-dwellers

Purrmaid

Half cat, half fish.

DISTRIBUTION: CORNWALL (UK)

(small subspecies identified in Skegness)

DIET: Fine tinned tuna/mackerel
Scrambled eggs on toast

Purrmaid called Fishkins discovered by P & B Wilde & has been disowned by family

Various colours & sizes

CLAW

Very Rare

Sea Monster

Large, peaceful & generally harmless

DISTRIBUTION: Pacific Ocean

DIET: seaweed, kelp, shrimps

* Known for wonderful singing

BLUE SPECKLED EGGS

FINS AID SWIMMING

SINGLE ROW OF TEETH

FRONT & BACK TEETH

Sea monsters collect shells to attract a mate

ᛕKᛞᛜᛝᚼᛞ KELPIE

FETLOCK COVERED IN SEAWEED FRONDS

Found in freshwater lakes. Very shy, docile & very fast

BABY KELPIE (FOAL)

DIET: grass, wildflowers
SIZE: 1m from flank to foot
DISTRIBUTION: SCOTLAND

ᛜ≈ᚠᛝᛏ᛭ᚦᛝ✕ᛥ PLOPTOPUS

POISONOUS SPIKES

Incredibly hostile — will attack on sight.

DISTRIBUTION: Frosty Sea, Deepest Dark of Deeps

SIZE: MASSIVE

50m long Ploptopus tried to eat my boat! I batted it on the head with my oar & knocked it out

Gertrude Wilde (91)

INK SACK

Nothing of any use. She slid off her bed and hopped across the floor to her desk. She had to hop because her room was a total mess. There were stacks of books piled on her armchair and the creaky wooden floor was covered in heaps of clothes and thick rugs. A couple of brilliantly coloured birds were roosting on top of her wardrobe, and a tank full of colour-changing newts perched precariously on her rickety bedside table.

Arranged along her windowsill were Indigo's treasures.

There was an ancient spearhead,
a lock of mermaid's hair, a battered
compass with funny markings
and a vial of rainbow-coloured
liquid. Indigo kept all these things
because you never knew when
they'd come in useful.

On the desk sat the postcard
they'd had from their parents a few
days before. Turning it over, Indigo
could see a craggy and inhospitable
mountain range in the Deepest
Dark of Deeps.

"Aha!" she squeaked, leaping back to the *Abracadarium* and turning to the section on mountain-dwelling Creatures. At the very end of the section, after the entries on trolls and wonder goats there was a page that was blank except for a note, scribbled in her mother's handwriting, that had been hastily stuck in with tape.

TO BE FOUND
Expedition number 2405:
Mogote Mountains/Deepest Dark of Deeps
Suspected NEW SPECIES
HIGHLY DANGEROUS

P & B Wilde

"This must be it!" Indigo said excitedly.

She couldn't wait to find out what sort of Creature it was. She tucked the *Abracadarium* under her arm and hurried to find Quigley. Between the two of them, they needed to get to the bottom of the mystery ...

... BEFORE
THERE
WERE
ANY
MORE
FLOODS.

—FIVE—

A CASE OF TINSELITIS

Indigo was nearly back in the kitchen when she heard a distant, muffled scraping noise. It was difficult to work out which direction the noise was coming from, but it was definitely getting louder. It wasn't coming from Fishkins' bathroom, or from the living room. She thought that maybe the yeti twins were knocking down the upstairs walls again, but she hadn't heard anything on her way down.

Indigo put the *Abracadarium* on the kitchen table and followed the sound all over the house, from floor to floor to floor, but just could not work out where it was coming from. She found Quigley dangling by one foot from a seventh-floor window, throwing fish to the nesting glamingos.

"There's a weird noise. I'm worried
it's our escapee up to no good again," she
explained, signing to her brother as she
hauled him inside. "I've just seen in the
Abracadarium that Mum and Dad have been
out in the Mogote Mountains looking for
a new Creature. It could be what's loose
in the house. Come on – I know you can't
hear, but you're so good at spotting things
when no one else does. Keep your eyes
peeled." She thought it was wise to leave out
the part that said the Creature was "highly
dangerous". Quigley always got overexcited
about anything that had more teeth or claws
than was strictly necessary.

They crept all over the house. Just as they
rounded the corner to the kitchen, Quigley
let out a great "Eeeek!" and pointed in alarm
to the door to the basement.

The basement was usually just a storage area for mountains of folded bedsheets, dragon toenail clippers, spare roller skates and boxes of Christmas decorations, but at the moment it also housed Graham the llama-corn. Graham had big bottom teeth that nearly touched his nose, a pink and yellow glittery horn poking out from his fringe of wild grey wool and an uncontrollable appetite. The llama-corn was very easily excited, and therefore also prone to the odd accident; Indigo had come downstairs one morning to the pungent bubblegum smell of llama-corn poo that took weeks to scrub out of the carpet. The living room still had a whiff of bubblegum about it even after she'd used Mrs Bristlebottom's Stubborn Stain and Stench Remover.

Indigo moved Graham upstairs after that,
but Graham had got peckish again one night
and eaten most of her mother's best dresses.
He had just started to munch on the curtains
when Indigo banished him to the basement.
He'd had terrible tummy ache (salsa dresses

are quite hard to digest) and was now only allowed to eat hay, which he was not AT ALL happy about.

Indigo pushed the basement door open slowly, listening for the strange muffled thumping; it was definitely louder down there. Quigley grabbed her hand and they tiptoed down the steps into the gloom, calling out to the llama-corn.

"Graham? Is it you making that noise?"

"Nope," said Graham through a mouthful of tattered multicoloured tinsel. "It's coming from up there." He looked towards the ceiling and swallowed the tinsel with a burp.

"Will you stop eating tinsel? You'll get tinselitis. Why don't you eat your nice hay?" Indigo said, distracted.

Quigley wandered around the room, looking at the ceiling.

"Hay is boring. Tinsel is zingy and zangy and makes my insides feel like fireworks!" said Graham, bouncing up and down with excitement.

"Yes, that's what I'm worried about," replied Indigo. "We do NOT want a repeat of the living-room-carpet fiasco."

Graham ignored her, slurping up a string of Christmas lights like a piece of spaghetti.

Indigo made a mental note to move the Christmas decorations to the loft, as Quigley tugged on her arm.

BANG BANG scuttle scuttle THUMP!

There it was again! Quigley pointed up at the ceiling. Something very strange was happening – a tiny hole was forming and it seemed to be getting bigger and bigger and bigger. It looked like something was chewing through the ceiling.

The trickle of falling plaster was followed by a chomping, nibbling, cracking sound. The llama-corn spat out a bauble and stared upwards as a huge crack spread across the ceiling.

There was a small pop, the light fitting fell out and a little white paw poked through the hole.

"Ut-oh!" said Graham, and with a FLOMP and a CREEEEEEEAAAAK and a flash of blue fire, the ceiling fell in.

-SIX-

A VISIT FROM MADAM GREY

CLANG CLANG,

the doorbell rang.

Indigo wiped the plaster from her eyes. It was in her hair, it was in her nose, it was even in her pockets. Through the clouds of dust, Indigo saw a small white blur vanish through the hole in the ceiling.

"The monster!" Indigo spluttered, spitting grit out of her mouth.

Quigley emerged from under a pile
of plaster, coughing and looking around
wildly. Indigo tugged him free and the pair
clambered from the wreckage and back up
the basement steps.

Indigo stumbled her way across the still
dripping hallway towards the front door and
the head-splitting clangs of the doorbell.
Brushing herself down, she opened the door
a crack, nervous that there might be another
monster waiting in the porch, but what she
saw was even worse. Madam Grey stood on
the step with her hands on her bony hips,
looking very cross indeed. Indigo gulped.
She would've preferred to find another
dragon on the doorstep.

Madam Grey was the head of the
local Neighbourhood Watch and she was
Terrifying with a capital T. She lived four

doors down at number 55, which was the
boxiest, most boring beige-brown house
on the whole street. She stalked
Jellybean Crescent as if she had a
thunder cloud hanging over
her head and shouted at
passing children for
"looking too happy"
and "walking in a
carefree manner".
She wore a
large pair of
binoculars
round her neck
so she could
spy on the
neighbours and
had a snappy,
yappy little dog

called Pebbles who she carried everywhere in a tiny bag.

Indigo pushed her face through the crack in the door and smiled as bravely as she dared.

"Hello, Madam Grey!" she said, trying to sound chirpy.

"What took you so long, girl?" Madam Grey snapped, spit landing on Indigo's nose.

"Sorry, I was ... er ... in the basement, sorting something out."

"Well I came by to see *what* all this racket is about.

And where has all this water come from?"
She waved a bony hand towards the dripping
trees and lamp posts. A soggy pigeon flapped
wetly on to the front gate. "Half the street is
flooded and I don't want to hear your infernal
noise on a Saturday morning – it makes
Pebbles very anxious. No respect for your
neighbours. Now where are your
parents?" She craned her neck
like an old, angry tortoise and
peered over Indigo's shoulder.

"Erm …" Indigo faltered, as the
pigeon opened its beak and chirped out a
stream of pink, soapy bubbles.

Madam Grey pushed the front door open
and strode inside number 47 as if she owned
the place. She barely had time to take in the
waterlogged hallway, the wreckage at the top
of the basement steps or Quigley, who was

swinging from the chandelier, with Olli and
Umpf dancing and laughing below, when
she was swept off her feet by Graham, who
was rocketing around
the house, powered

70

by tinsel and covered in ceiling plaster.

"NO!" shouted Indigo, horrified.

"AARRGGHHHHHHHHH!" shrieked Madam Grey, as the llama-corn bounced her around the living room, up the stairs and back down into the kitchen. "WHAT IS HAPPENING?" she wailed, as Graham bounced her far too high. She flew through the air, landing on her bottom with a big squelchy SPLAT in a giant pile of rainbow-coloured llama-corn poo.

"Indigo Wilde! WHAT is this hideous mess and *WHERE* are your parents?" Madam Grey hissed with terrifying anger. Luckily, it seemed she didn't recognise llama-corn poo (she wasn't the sort to recognise anything remotely magical) so Indigo decided to ignore that part of the question, but how could she tell Madam Grey that her parents were currently halfway up the Mogote Mountains? Madam Grey had probably never even heard of the Deepest Dark of Deeps and would probably just think Indigo was making up stories. Madam Grey hadn't believed Indigo that time a visiting giant had accidentally stood on her car. She had accused Indigo of "telling nasty little lies".

Indigo didn't really fancy explaining all the Creatures to Madam Grey, either. The awful woman was *just* the sort who would be terrified of even the smallest magical thing and would probably report Indigo, or her parents, to the police or some other People In Charge, and the last thing Indigo wanted was for her Creature friends to be locked up in cages, or for Quigley and her to have to go back to living in the Unknown Wilderness.

"Errr … they've just … popped out," Indigo said as convincingly as she could.

"Well, I am going to sit right here and wait for them to come back so I can talk to them about your DEVILISH behaviour," snapped Madam Grey, wiping her clothes down and plonking herself down at the kitchen table, stroking her horrible whimpering little dog.

Indigo grimaced. This was the last thing she needed. Now there were two uninvited monsters in the house.

"And can't you control that … that …
what *is* that animal?" asked Madam Grey,
staring at Graham, who was jumping up and
down on the sofa with what looked like
another pair of Queenie's bloomers hanging
out of his mouth.

"Oh, erm … that's just a llama …" said
Indigo hurriedly, shooing Graham quickly
out of the room before the llama-corn
spotted Madam Grey's very shiny, very
edible-looking shoes, and before Madam
Grey noticed the llama-corn's sparkling
horn.

Luckily, the rest of her Creature friends
had had the sense to make themselves scarce
and, anyway, it seemed Madam Grey really
was one of those people who was incapable
of noticing anything extraordinary or
magical, even if it was jumping up and down

under her nose chewing a pair of frilly pink knickers.

"I'm not even going to ask why you have a llama in your house. Crackpots, the lot of you," the old woman muttered, scratching Pebbles under his chin. "Now, make me a cup of tea. Pebbles will have a cup, too. And hurry up about it."

Indigo made Madam Grey and her horrible dog a cup of tea and sat down nervously at the table, tucking the *Abracadarium* out of sight under the tea cosy and trying to act normal.

As Indigo nervously arranged biscuits on a plate, she thought that this morning had already gone from bad to worse. Little did she know, things were about to go from worse to even worser.

- SEVEN -

WHEN THINGS GOT WORSER

Pebbles was not a nice dog. He looked a bit like a feather duster that had been sat on and he was about as friendly as a dragon with toothache. If children tried to pet him in the street, he would growl and snap, and if anyone annoyed his beloved Madam Grey, he would bite their ankles.

Pebbles was spoilt and rotten and about as not-nice as a dog could get. But Pebbles was also a total and utter scaredy-pants. He was scared of many things, but his Top Three Things To Be Avoided At All Costs were:

THE POSTMAN
SQUIRRELS
SUDDEN NOISES

So it was a little unfortunate for Pebbles that at the exact moment Madam Grey had stopped cuddling and cooing over him to drink her tea, there came an almighty BOOM from the floor above.

Several things happened at once: plaster dust dropped from the ceiling and coated them all with a fine powder; Quigley fell from the chandelier, spraying them with sparkling shards of glass; and Graham came skidding back into the room, chased by Queenie, who was yelling "GIVE ME BACK THOSE BLOOMERS, YOU ROTTEN BEAST!"

All of this sent Pebbles into a mad frenzy. He leapt from Madam Grey's arms, yapping and snarling, and ran straight for the llama-corn, who leapt from sofa to chair to table in panic, knocking Madam Grey's tea on to Queenie, who roared with anger.

BOOM.

BOOM.

BOOM.

"What is going on?" cried Madam Grey, as Pebbles yelped and snarled, narrowly missing Graham's leg and sinking his horrible little teeth into a cushion instead, feathers flying everywhere.

"I'll be back in a second! Just … just … stay there!" yelled Indigo as she sprinted from the room and up the stairs, Quigley following just behind.

At first, Indigo thought – or hoped – she'd imagined the noise, but there it was again, louder, and this time with an added TA-ROOO TA-ROOO.

STOMP.

STOMP.

STOMP.

It was coming from the library.

Indigo hoisted Quigley on to her shoulders and ran down the hall, throwing open the library doors.

The library was huge and echoey and the noise from inside was deafening.

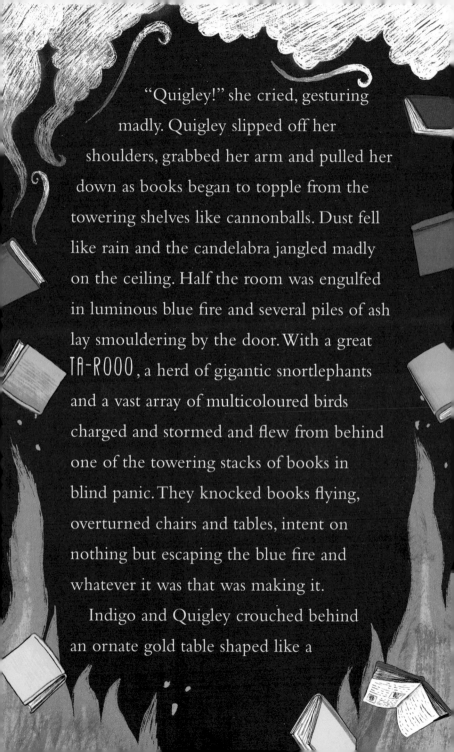

"Quigley!" she cried, gesturing madly. Quigley slipped off her shoulders, grabbed her arm and pulled her down as books began to topple from the towering shelves like cannonballs. Dust fell like rain and the candelabra jangled madly on the ceiling. Half the room was engulfed in luminous blue fire and several piles of ash lay smouldering by the door. With a great TA-ROOO, a herd of gigantic snortlephants and a vast array of multicoloured birds charged and stormed and flew from behind one of the towering stacks of books in blind panic. They knocked books flying, overturned chairs and tables, intent on nothing but escaping the blue fire and whatever it was that was making it.

Indigo and Quigley crouched behind an ornate gold table shaped like a centaur carrying a tea tray. Then, with a growl and a grunt, the yeti twins appeared in the doorway.

"WE HELP! NO WORRY, INDIGO AND QUIG!" they roared, and before Indigo could shout "NO!" they ran straight into the pandemonium. They tried their very best to herd the terrified Creatures back through the library and away from the hallway and the staircase (and the wrath of Madam Grey), but their flailing and roaring was making matters worse. One snortlephant reared up on its hind legs and knocked a hole in the ceiling with its huge curved tusks as Olli gave a loud "ROOOAR!" The birds shrieked even louder when Umpf tried to shoo them in the other direction with her large clawed hands.

Just as Indigo jumped up and yelled "STOP!",
she saw a familiar white blur out of the
corner of her eye, right under the feet of the
stampeding snortlephants. It had to be the
monster again! Before she could get a good
look at it, it was gone in a flash of blue.

All the yelling in the world wouldn't

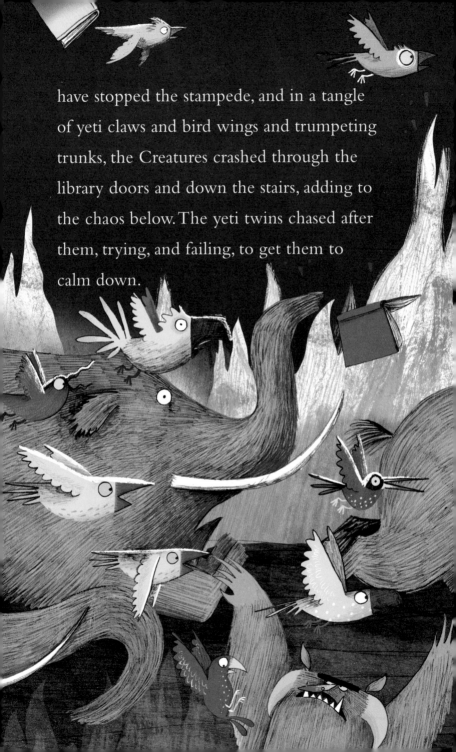

have stopped the stampede, and in a tangle of yeti claws and bird wings and trumpeting trunks, the Creatures crashed through the library doors and down the stairs, adding to the chaos below. The yeti twins chased after them, trying, and failing, to get them to calm down.

Indigo winced as she heard the terrified yells of Madam Grey and the frenzied yapping of Pebbles, but she needed to see if she could find out where that mysterious white blur had disappeared to. Hoping that Olli and Umpf might eventually get things under control, Indigo took Quigley's hand and they dashed down the hall as calmly as they could.

Just as they reached the end of the corridor, Madam Grey appeared at the top of the staircase, blocking their way. She looked as furious as a rhinoceros with a head cold and was covered top-to-toe in cushion feathers, like a human-sized chicken.

"INDIGO WILDE!" she screeched, storming towards Indigo and Quigley, but before she could utter another word, a gigantic, sparkling and bejewelled glamingo swooped in from the open library doors, picked Madam Grey up in its beak and flew straight out of a smashed window on the landing. Quigley clapped and cheered.

They could hear Madam Grey's warbling shrieks as the bird flew her round and round the house and watched as the glamingo eventually came to rest on the seventh-floor roof, deposited Madam Grey in its nest, sat on her head and promptly laid a ginormous egg.

Indigo gulped and squeezed Quigley's hand. There was no way Madam Grey could *not* have noticed that the house was full of magical Creatures by now.

Surely it was only a
matter of time before she
called the police.

-EIGHT-
THE STINK OF A STONK

Trying not to think about what would happen when the police were called, Indigo and Quigley carried on creeping down the hallway. The white shape flashed out in front of them and round the corner, leaving a faint trail of smoke. They chased after it and watched as it disappeared through an old curtain and up the hidden staircase behind it that led to the second floor. Indigo burst through the curtain and took the stairs two

by two, but she simply wasn't quick enough. When they emerged on to the landing above, there was no sign of the monster.

"It's got to be here *somewhere*," Indigo breathed, as they tiptoed down the echoey second-floor hallway.

There were thirty-two rooms on the second floor, and each one was home to a different Creature. The third room on the right, for example, housed a sea monster. You'd never have guessed you were still inside a house if you'd peeked through the door – instead of carpet there was beautiful white sand and gently lapping turquoise water that stretched from wall to wall. No matter the time of day, the room was bathed in the orange light of sunset. There were rock pools and seaweed and the smell of salt and fish. The sea monster herself could usually be seen sitting high on a rock, playing guitar and singing unidentifiable songs terribly out of tune.

The turret room at the end of the hallway was home to a troupe of flying monkeys. Indigo made sure to always shut their door behind her quickly, because the last time the monkeys had escaped from the house she had spent a week chasing them all over town, trying to stop them stealing the neighbours' washing and flying in through people's windows to eat their roast dinners.

But it wasn't the door to the sea monster's beach or to the flying monkey chamber that was open now … It was much, much worse than that.

"Quigley – go and get Queenie, we're going to need some help," Indigo gulped.

The door to the twenty-fifth room on

the left stood wide open. In fact, on closer inspection, it had been completely smashed off its hinges. Indigo peered cautiously round the door frame. Inside, it was raining and the room was full of thick undergrowth and the overpowering stench of rotten cabbages.

Pinching her nose, Indigo stepped into the room. The smell seemed to be coming from a large, quivering bush in the corner.

"It's OK, Stonk," choked Indigo, trying not to retch. "You can come out. I think the monster has gone."

Nervously emerging from between the leaves came an extremely odd Creature. It looked a bit like a skunk, but it was about ten times the size and its fur rippled with different colours. It was almost as if its coat was *made* of rainbows. It wore a small, black bowler hat and a polka-dot bow tie, and shuffled out of the bushes holding a fine gentleman's walking cane. On top of its squirrel-ish head grew a pair of glowing horns and every now and then, the stonk snorted and emitted a cloud of rainbow-coloured, cabbage-smelling gas.

"Did you see which way it—" But before Indigo could cough out her question, a white blur shot out of the undergrowth and the stonk gave a ginormous, panicked SNORT and filled the room with a colourful cabbagey cloud. Indigo couldn't see a thing and neither could the stonk.

He crashed around in panic, puffing out more rainbow gas.

Somehow Indigo managed to feel her way back to the smashed door and threw herself

on to the landing, coughing and rubbing her eyes.

"Are you OK, Indigo? Quigley said you were in trouble," said a gravelly voice from the middle of the rainbow fog.

"Queenie! Thank goodness!" Indigo spluttered. Goblins had no sense of smell (how else would they be able to eat rotten fish stew for dinner?) so Queenie was the best person for this job.

"I can't see a thing! And the *smell*!" coughed Indigo, trying to waft away the suffocatingly stinky rainbow fog.

"It's all right. I've got an idea," said the goblin in her slow, earthy voice. And the next thing Indigo knew, the hallway was filled with flying monkeys, flapping excitedly through the fog.

"What sort of a plan is this?" Indigo

shouted as a monkey
flew straight into her head.
"Ah!" replied Queenie.
"Wrong door ... I thought that one

was the cleaning cupboard. I was going to get the hoover out and suck all the fog up."

"Erm …" said Indigo, trying not to sound too exasperated.

"I can help!" came an excitable voice from amidst the cloud.

"Graham? Is that you?" called Indigo with a groan, her heart sinking. Queenie growled.

"Yes, hello!" replied the llama-corn, appearing at her side. "It does smell a bit, doesn't it? I'm sure if I jumped about lots and lots, like this …" And the llama-corn sprang from wall to wall, knocking great chunks out of the plaster and causing the bust of a bearded,

bespectacled lady to topple through a
window.

"NO! No! It's OK, Gr—" But Indigo
was cut off by the sea monster poking her
head out of her door, crying, "Can someone
PLEASE open a window *or five*. It absolutely
stinks up here!"

Indigo and Queenie stumbled about,
opening all the windows along the landing
and slowly the stench and the rainbow-
coloured cloud dispersed.

Indigo blinked and looked around.
"Where's Stonk?" she asked nervously.

"I think I smell him that way," replied
Graham, pointing down the stairs with his
hoof.

Indigo sighed. She could only imagine
the carnage that would be waiting for her
downstairs, but it would have to wait. She

could hear the now familiar sound of the monster's thumping and scratching coming from the floor above.

"Queenie, find Stonk and try to calm him down. I've got to catch this monster before it causes any more trouble," Indigo said. She bounded up the nearest staircase and just caught sight of the white flash shooting through another open door. The door to …

"NOT MY BEDROOM!"

she groaned.

-NINE-
THE CHOCOLATE THIEF

As Indigo reached her bedroom, she caught a glimpse of white vanishing under her bed. The birds squawked and hooted madly from the top of her wardrobe.

"Shhhhhh," she comforted quietly, and the birds fell silent, rustling their feathers nervously.

Indigo didn't like to admit it, but she was a bit scared too. She wished Quigley was up here with her. But this was her chance to to call for backup.

She looked at the giant family portrait above her bed for reassurance, steeling herself as she crept towards the sound of snuffling and munching. She slowly reached out a hand and pulled up the duvet, peering under the bed. There was nothing there … except the big box she kept all her chocolate in. The box had been overflowing with treats, but now it was empty save for a few chewed wrappers and a single half-eaten chocolate bar.

CHOCOLATE *finest* DARK CHOC yum

"It's eaten all my chocolate!" she gasped, turning to see a streak of blue fire disappearing out of the door.

The birds started squawking madly again as a loud thump and a TA-ROOOOOO! sounded several floors below. Without a breath, Indigo ran to see what new trouble the monster was about to get her into, pocketing the half-eaten chocolate bar on the way ...

-TEN-

HOW TO CATCH A MONSTER

Indigo had never seen such a scene of devastation. The snortlephants were trumpeting and crashing around the kitchen, knocking plates and chairs all over the place. The flying monkeys were raiding the fridge and hurling tubs of beetroot and potato salad at Graham, who was bouncing round and round the room, catching the food in his mouth and swallowing it whole. Queenie chased after the llama-corn, still yelling about her ruined bloomers. The multicoloured birds were zooming all over the place, squawking their beaks off and creating such strong gusts of wind with their wings that a small tornado had formed in the hallway and sucked up half the furniture.

The yeti twins had forgotten all about rounding the Creatures up and were happily knocking down the wall into the bathroom, and Fishkins was meowing loudly in protest. Meanwhile, the trolls kept leaping up in excitement from their seats on the exploding water pipes so that water burst out in fountains and drenched Fishkins all over again.

There was a thick fog of stinky, rainbow-coloured gas lying over the whole scene, as the stonk quivered under the table, his bowler hat over his eyes. Quigley was practising his cartwheels, laughing gleefully at the chaos and in the living room, buried under an avalanche of cushion feathers, was a terrified, whimpering Pebbles.

In the midst of the pandemonium, Madam Grey appeared at the door, looking like she had been dragged through several hedges backwards. Her clothes were torn and tatty where she had clearly slid down the roofs of the house, she had egg dripping down her face and one shoe missing.

She stumbled into the room in a confused daze, snatched up Pebbles and fled from the house, muttering darkly about hoodlums and calling the police. Indigo would have to worry about her later. She needed to fix this mess first.

Indigo took the biggest, deepest breath she had ever taken.

"EVERYONE STOP!" she yelled at the very top of her voice.

For once everyone listened. The crashing and trumpeting and howling and meowing and hammering and swinging stopped. But in the middle of the silence there was a small snuffle, the pile of feathers shuddered and jiggled and wiggled, and "*AAAACHOOOOOOOOO!*", out of the feathers shot a Creature. A white, fluffy Creature. A white, fluffy, fanged Creature who sneezed out a ball of bright blue fire that singed Queenie's eyebrows off.

"THE MONSTER!" they all shouted in unison.

Startled by the sudden noise and before anyone could get a proper look at it, the Creature vanished in a puff of dark blue smoke.

There was a great rush of movement as
all the Creatures prepared to lose their heads
again, but Indigo shouted "STOOOOOOP!"
and silence fell once more.

"LISTEN." She snatched the *Abracadarium*
from the kitchen table, signing so that
everyone could understand.
"The *Abracadarium*
says that our mum
and dad are on an
expedition in
the mountains
looking for a
new and highly
dangerous Creature."

Quigley's eyes lit
up and he made his
gnashing-toothed
monster face.

"Whatever this monster is," Indigo carried on, ignoring him, "it loves chocolate. It's eaten my entire stash." She held up the half-eaten chocolate bar. "But it's really fast and I think it can make itself *invisible*. We just need to lure it out somehow and then GRAB it. Any ideas?"

Quigley nodded and jumped up and down, pointing first to the chocolate in Indigo's hand and then to the collapsed steps to the basement. Indigo followed him, glancing nervously out of the hallway window to check that the police hadn't arrived yet. It was only a matter of time; Madam Grey would have called them by now.

Under the rubble of the basement ceiling, Quigley unearthed the big fishing net that they'd once used to rescue a mermaid from a well and laid it on the hallway floor. Everyone helped to cover it with a thick blanket of feathers, while Quigley signed his orders to the birds. Then Indigo put the half-eaten chocolate bar in the middle of the disguised net, and they all slunk back into the shadows to watch and wait.

They waited for so long that Indigo's bottom got pins and needles, but eventually the telltale snuffling and munching noises of the monster became louder. The feathers jiggled and wiggled and then – SNAP! – the chocolate bar vanished in one big MUNCH.

"NOW!" yelled Indigo, and with a great heave from all the Creatures, and the FLAP FLAP FLAP of hundreds of birds' wings, the net swept upwards and the monster was trapped inside. There was silence.

"Is that *it*?" said Queenie.

-ELEVEN-
HAYSTACKS

It was a rabbit. A cute, fluffy, white bunny rabbit with black spots on its back, a soft, pink wiffling nose and two very large front teeth. It blinked its dark eyes innocently at Indigo and licked the chocolate from around its mouth.

A feather floated from the sky and tickled the bunny's nose. "ACHOOO!" it sneezed, and blue flames shot from its mouth.

"Hello," said Indigo cautiously. "Erm … what are you?"

"I'm a wabbit," said the rabbit, in a twitchy sort of voice.

"I can see that, but … do you have a name?" replied Indigo, feeling absolutely exhausted.

"Ah, yes. My name is Haystacks."

Indigo sighed. "You've made a bit of a mess of the house, you know. Do you think you might … settle down and relax a bit now? I gather you like chocolate."

The rabbit nodded so vigorously his eyes boggled in his head. "I could smell chocolate somewhere in the house and I've been looking for it. Finally found it under a bed. Delicious." A dreamy, satisfied look came over the rabbit's face.

Indigo noticed several scraps of grubby, crumpled paper stuck to the rabbit's fur, in amongst the chocolate and bits of straw. It was the missing pieces of her mother's note.

Dear Indigo,

Very hot here. Found this adorable new creature in the deepest dark crevasses of the Mogote Mountains. He told us he was once a family pet, but he was left out in the wilderness after he accidentally chewed a hole straight through the fridge door to get at the chocolate mousse inside.

He's really easy to care for. Just feed him chocolate on the hour, every hour, or he gets a bit destructive. He can move lightning fast and we think he might be able to become invisible. Fascinating! Update the Abracadarium when you can.

Your father has sunburn on his ears and is doing quite a bit of grumbling. We'll be home soon.

Have fun!

Love, Mum and Dad x

Indigo laughed a little bit hysterically and put the note in her pocket.

"Right, Haystacks," she said, "let's get you some lunch."

But as Indigo turned to head into the kitchen, she caught sight of Madam Grey through the window. She was barking down her phone and hopping madly around the garden, jumping every time one of the plants made a snap for her ankles. Indigo's tummy lurched, thinking about Haystacks and all the other Creatures that would be locked away in cages, if Madam Grey had her way …

INDIGO WAS DETERMINED NOT TO LET THAT HAPPEN.

-TWELVE-
THE INGENIOUS PLAN

Number 47 was in a sorry state. Once
Indigo had found a supply of chocolate for
Haystacks, they all set about the mammoth
task of repairing the house. There were
floors to be repaired, walls to be rebuilt and
new cushions to make. Queenie was so busy
with the sewing machine her claws were a
blur.

Luckily, the yetis and trolls were quite
good with a hammer and even Fishkins lent

a paw to patch up the pipework. On top of all the DIY, Indigo and Quigley had to make sure Haystacks had his chocolate fix every hour and that Graham wasn't allowed within ten metres of any Christmas decorations after he had ruined the living-room carpet for a third time.

While they scrubbed, hammered and plastered, Indigo and Quigley were trying to come up with an Ingenious Plan. They knew Madam Grey wasn't going to take her defeat lying down and they had to protect the Creatures in their care.

At teatime the next day Indigo and Quigley were just sitting down to a large jam roll baked by Olli when the doorbell rang.

It had to be the police. Indigo opened the door with a shaky hand and put on her brightest smile.

Chief Inspector Pudding and Sergeant Plum seemed totally unaware of the biting daisies chomping on their shoelaces.

"Oh, hello, Inspector. Sergeant," said Indigo confidently. "Everything OK?"

"We've had a report from a member of the public regarding this residence," Chief Inspector Pudding said, peering down from underneath her tall, shiny hat.

"Oh," Indigo said, pretending to look confused. "Let me get my mum and dad."

She hurried out of sight and returned with Queenie the goblin and Olli the yeti, who were dressed very convincingly in things they'd found in Bertram's and Philomena's wardrobes. Olli wore a faded blue suit, a yellow bow tie and a straw hat, and had fashioned himself a moustache

from some of Graham's wool. Queenie
was wearing a lurid pink salsa dress, a pair
of mismatched wellington boots and a
huge powder-blue wig bedecked
with bells, bows and
an ornamental
pineapple.

The wig was so tall it kept bashing into the ceiling.

"Oh, hello, Inspector Pudding! Good morning, Sergeant Plum!" Queenie cried in her melodic voice.

"UGGGGG," said Olli.

"Erm … good … good morning!" exclaimed Chief Inspector Pudding, gazing in astonishment at the towering wig and the wool moustache.

"Errm … y-y-yes, well … as the chief inspector said," Sergeant Plum stammered as Queenie's wig threatened to knock half the vases off the hallway shelf, "w-w-w-we received an

anonymous t-t-t-tip-off from the p-p-p-public that there were children in this house who had been left home alone w-w-w-without adult s-s-s-supervision. And also ..." He glanced at the chief inspector, who was still staring at the pair.

"Yes, also," continued the chief inspector, standing up straight and looking stern, "reports of a variety of dangerous animals being housed here."

Queenie chuckled in her most carefree manner and Olli gave a booming laugh that sounded more like a roar.

"Come and have a look around, officers," said Queenie, ushering them inside. They marched around the house, opening doors and looking in cupboards, with Indigo and Quigley trailing after them. All through the ground floor and up to the first floor there was not a dragon or a goblin or a single fairy to be found.

As they reached the end of the corridor on the first floor, Indigo held her breath. If they discovered the hidden door behind the curtain, all was lost. The second floor was so full of Creatures that there was no hiding them.

Just as the officers drew near the curtain, Quigley burst into action with some enthusiastic cartwheels, ending with a flourish at the top of the stairs and smiling his most winning smile.

Sergeant Plum clapped.

"What a lovely little brother you have, young lady," chuckled Chief Inspector Pudding. "You must be very proud of him."

Indigo gave Quigley a tight hug. They both crossed their fingers behind their backs for luck as they followed the officers down

the stairs and into the hall.

"Well," Chief Inspector Pudding continued, "this all seems to be in order. Sorry for wasting your time. Oh! What a sweet pet bunny rabbit you have, too," she added, bending down to scoop up Haystacks from where he had just appeared on the front doormat. Indigo and Quigley looked at each other in panic.

"Careful with that bunny, officers, he has a nasty bite!" chimed Queenie, hurriedly taking Haystacks (who had begun to smoulder slightly at the whiskers). With her large clawed hand, Queenie ushered the police officers out of the front door.

Chief Inspector Pudding and Sergeant Plum gave Queenie, Olli and the rabbit one last suspicious look, before finally strolling away from the house.

They'd just turned the corner and disappeared from view behind a hedge when Haystacks set fire to the doormat.

As Indigo and Quigley waved them off they saw Madam Grey across the street, binoculars to her eyes. She was staring straight at number 47, Pebbles quivering in his little bag.

Indigo and Quigley waved and laughed, shutting the door on her disbelieving face as the police officers walked casually away down the street.

"You can all come out now!" cried Indigo.

Fairies emerged from the folds of curtains, the stonk shuffled out from under the dining table and the flying monkeys flapped out from the lampshades. The pixies stopped pretending to be stuffed toys and jumped up

and down with joy. Umpf climbed out from
inside the grandfather clock and hundreds
of birds flocked from inside vases, behind
cushions and under sofas.

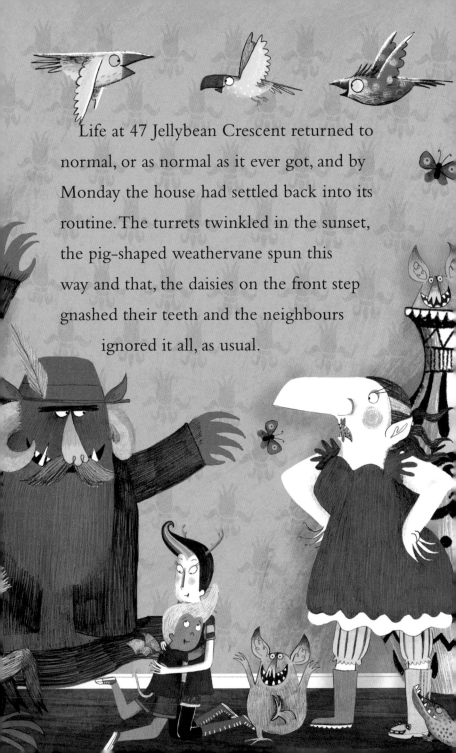

Life at 47 Jellybean Crescent returned to normal, or as normal as it ever got, and by Monday the house had settled back into its routine. The turrets twinkled in the sunset, the pig-shaped weathervane spun this way and that, the daisies on the front step gnashed their teeth and the neighbours ignored it all, as usual.

THEN, ON THURSDAY,
THE DOORBELL RANG ...

CLANG CLANG

Mountain-dwellers

TROLL

Very mischievous, always up to no good.
Small to medium size. Adu[lt]
male approx. 50cm high.
Baby trolls are only bor[n] [un]der
a full moon.

DISTRIBUTION: Mou[ntain] ranges worldwide

DIET: Moss, toads[...], insects & berries

large e[ars]
can jump very high

ALSO LIKE [cru]MPETS [&] INDIGO w[...]

WON[DE]R GOA[T]

Elusive [cre]ature coveted [...]
and thi[...] cold resistant co[...]

DISTRIB[UT]ION:
Ice m[oun]tains
Dee[pes]t Dark
of [D]eeps

DIET: snowberries

Destruction of
snowberry forests has
led to massive decline
in Wonder Goat population

can be [white] or grey
thick coat
solid gold
[sn]owbern[...]

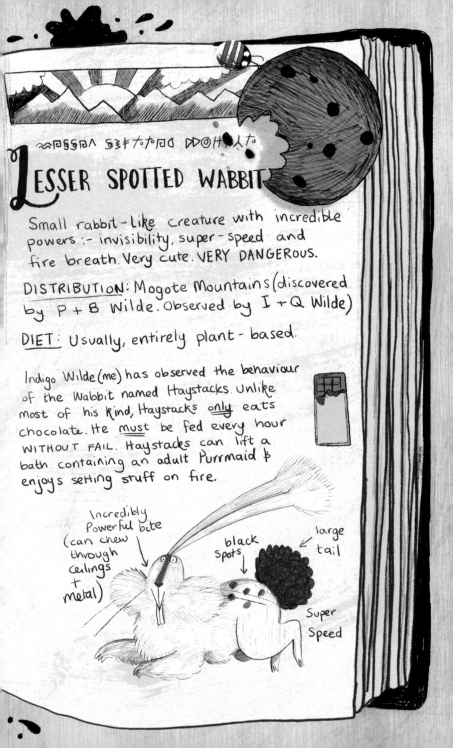

LESSER SPOTTED WABBIT

Small rabbit-like creature with incredible powers :- invisibility, super-speed and fire breath. Very cute. VERY DANGEROUS.

DISTRIBUTION: Mogote Mountains (discovered by P + B Wilde. Observed by I + Q Wilde)

DIET: Usually, entirely plant-based.

Indigo Wilde (me) has observed the behaviour of the Wabbit named Haystacks. Unlike most of his kind, Haystacks <u>only</u> eats chocolate. He <u>must</u> be fed every hour WITHOUT FAIL. Haystacks can lift a bath containing an adult Purrmaid & enjoys setting stuff on fire.

Incredibly Powerful bite (can chew through ceilings + metal)

black spots

large tail

Super Speed

THIS LITTLE BUG GUY
GETS EVERYWHERE.
EACH TIME YOU TURN
THE PAGE AND SEE A
PICTURE, SEE IF YOU
CAN FIND HIM.

ACKNOWLEDGEMENTS

Hello! My name is Pippa and I wrote this book, and drew the pictures. I hope you enjoyed reading it as much as I enjoyed making it.

We all know how important it is to say thank you when someone does something nice, so I would like to say thank you very very much to YOU ... for buying, or borrowing, this book – and for reading it. When I was a bit smaller than I am now, I dreamed of writing my own stories, so the very fact you're reading this has made my dreams come true. Maybe you would like to make books, too? I think you'd be brilliant at it; just remember, if you have a great idea for a story, make sure you write it down before it oozes out of your head.

There are lots of amazing people who have worked very hard to turn my words and pictures into an actual, real-life book and I'd like to say thank you to them, too:

Claire, my agent, who always champions my ideas and gives me unwavering support – thank you times a squillion.

Rachel, who does a fabulous job making sure all my full stops are in the right place and double-checks I haven't waffled on for pages and pages and pages. Alison, who makes everything look tip-top and doesn't get cross when I send her a million and one changes. And Amina, thank you for all your brilliant help.

A big thank you to the teams at HCG who work tirelessly to show my books to all the wonderful co-ed publishers and booksellers across the Known and Unknown lands.

And very lastly, but not very leastly, I'd like to thank my family — because without them I wouldn't exist, and if I didn't exist I wouldn't be able to hold a pencil.

My eternal gratitude to my parents, who brought me up surrounded by books and gave me the invaluable gift of imagination. And to my brother and sister, who filled my childhood with utter joy and a healthy dose of weirdness.

Humongous thanks to Ben, who has always believed in every one of my crazy ideas ... except for my conveyor-belt road idea, which he says is silly. And thank you to my children, Roux and Autumn, for providing endless inspiration for Indigo and Quigley. I hope you love this book, because I wrote it especially for you.

Thank you, you are all marvellous.

Pippa Curnick

LOOK OUT FOR INDIGO'S NEXT
AMAZING ADVENTURE IN...